THE LOVE TRIALS

BOOK THREE

J.S. COOPER & HELEN COOPER

This book is a work of fiction. Names, characters, places, and incidents either are the product of the author's imagination or are used fictitiously. Any resemblance to actual persons, living or dead, events, or locales is entirely coincidental.

THE LOVE TRIALS

BOOK THREE

PROLOGUE

"Do you take Nancy Hastings to be your lawfully wedded wife?" The priest spoke loudly and clearly, nodding at me with a small smile as he waited for my answer. I stared at him for a second, my voice mute and my heart beating. I knew that whatever I decided to do would mean the downfall of someone.

As I stood there, I thought to myself that the question shouldn't be what would you do for love? The question should be what wouldn't you do? What wouldn't you do, means a whole lot more. Trust me, I know. For love I'd walk to hell and back. I'd climb a mountain. I'd swim an ocean. I'd jump over valleys and swing through jungles. For love, I'd give my life. But that's not the question upon me now. The question upon me now is, would I walk away? Would I leave her standing at the altar because I love her? Did I love her enough to not marry her?

That, my dears, is the ultimate question and I had no idea what to do.

I looked at Nancy then, standing in her white wedding dress, and I knew in that moment that marrying her wouldn't be right. It would be the ultimate betrayal of everything I stood for.

CHAPTER ONE

Jaxon

There's a problem with selling your soul to the devil. It often turns out that his terms aren't as favorable as he leads you to believe. It should be obvious, right? You make a deal with the devil, you're asking for trouble, right? But, how do you say no to the devil, if he's your father? I don't know a man alive who doesn't want to win his father's approval.

When I walked into my room and saw Brandon and Greyson waiting for me, I was worried, sad, but not totally surprised. In fact, part of me wondered what had taken so long for them to arrive. My father had expected them to show up within hours of Nancy's arrival. Though he hadn't counted on Nancy being so headstrong. Neither had I.

"Jaxon." Brandon's lip curled at me. "You messed with the wrong man this time."

"I don't think so." My voice was low as I stared into his face. His eyes were narrowed and full of hate.

"I didn't know you were fighting Daddy's battles for him now."

"I'm not sure why you and lover-boy are here." I turned from Brandon to Greyson, and smirked. "Don't tell me you guys are ready to publicly declare your love for each other?"

"You're a punk, little boy." Greyson's eyes were cold as he stared at me. "You do know Brandon has a gun?"

"I do have eyes." I stared at the gun in Brandon's hand. So cold and small; it was such an ironic thing that such an insignificant object could end a life. One shot, one bullet, one life gone. It was as simple as that.

Greyson shook his head as he stared at me. I could see from his expression that he was furious; though he wasn't murderous. The murderous look was coming from Brandon.

"So, you going to kill me?" I walked towards Brandon and the gun. "You going to take my life?"

"Is that what you want?" Brandon moved the gun up.

"No," I said, shaking my head and smiling slowly. "That's not what I want."

"I didn't think so." Brandon tilted his head and looked at me for a few seconds. I swallowed as I saw him adjust the gun in his hand. I guess I was more nervous than I thought.

"What do you want, Brandon?" I stared at him with a bored expression.

"I want to know why you brought my daughter into it?"

"I don't know what you're talking about." I shrugged and ran my hands through my hair casually.

"Nancy, why is she here?"

"She applied to the academy." I smiled sweetly. "I guess she wanted to learn about love…" I paused and stared directly into his eyes. "Or maybe she wanted to learn about sex."

"You son of a bitch."

"Thanks." I nodded and smiled, hiding my hatred of the man in front of me. The only reason I didn't deck him was because I knew that wasn't what my father wanted. I also knew that Nancy would never forgive me if I beat her dad up. I wasn't sure why I cared so much about what she thought, but I did.

"You really want to play with fire, Jaxon?" Greyson took a step towards me. "You really sure about this?"

"What are you? Good cop?" I rolled my eyes. "Nancy came to the academy by herself." I shrugged. "She's into one of our teachers here."

"Who?" Brandon's lips curled up in disgust.

"Hunter; he used to teach at her high school." I yawned. "Can you leave now?"

"Have you touched my daughter?" Brandon's eyes narrowed.

"Yes." I grinned at him. "She's very sweet."

"You piece of…" Brandon charged towards me and Greyson held him back.

"Careful, Brandon." Greyson continued holding him back. "You don't want to do something you'll regret. He's not worth it."

"You wouldn't want to kill your grandchild's father, would you?" The words slipped out of my mouth easily. The missile had been launched.

"Grandchild?" Brandon gasped and I watched his face pale. "You slept with her?"

"What do you think?" I asked him softly and stared him down, my heart beating fast as I saw his hand tighten on the gun.

"I think that's the last time you'll make that mistake." He moved forward and pulled the trigger back. All I heard next was *bang*.

CHAPTER TWO

Nancy

I was scared to find out who had died. It didn't seem real to me. In a way, I didn't want to know. I was conflicted about my feelings. Conflicted and confused. I knew that between Jaxon and Hunter, there was one I'd prefer to still be alive. I wasn't sure if that made me cruel or inhumane. I knew that if it came to it and it was up to me, I'd rather Jaxon still be alive. I wasn't sure what that said about me.

"Who's dead?" I whispered to Amber as I followed her into the study.

"You don't know?" She raised an eyebrow at me and studied my face. "Shit, you really don't know."

"That's right, I don't know," I snapped at her. "I just got in, how would I know?"

"Where've you been?" She continued to study my face and I shook my head at her.

"I was walking," I said and then sighed. My body was beginning to shake and I knew that I wasn't going to be able to stand the stress of not knowing. "Who died?"

"You mean who was murdered?" Amber's eyes gleamed at me and a part of me wondered if she wasn't excited by what had happened.

"Why do you sound so gleeful?"

"What are you talking about, Nancy?" She frowned at me. "Why would I sound gleeful that someone was dead? Are you hearing things?"

"I'm not hearing anything you're not saying," I muttered. "Your tone sounds like…"

"Nancy, there you are." Louise rushed through the door and up to me. "The police want to talk to you."

"To me?" I frowned. "Why?"

"There's been an unfortunate accident."

Amber spoke up. "That was no accident."

"Amber." Louise cut her off with a frown and Amber turned away with pursed lips.

"What's going on, exactly?"

"It appears that he's been shot." Louise looked at me with downcast eyes. "I'm not really sure why."

"Her name was on a note in his hand," Amber muttered and I could feel my hand itching to slap her.

"Who is dead?" I shouted. I'd had enough of the cat and mouse game of knowing. Who was dead?

"Hunter." Louise looked devastated. "He was one of our best teachers."

"Hunter." I felt my shoulders sagging as I realized Jaxon was safe. I knew that I had issues. I knew that everything wasn't right. And a part of me wondered if Jaxon had killed Hunter. I didn't even know what he was capable of doing. He'd acted kind of crazy in the club. He'd acted as if he were capable of punching Hunter or hurting him badly. He'd acted jealous and mean and I knew that he wasn't thrilled that I'd had a crush on him. However, I wasn't sure why he would kill Hunter for that? It didn't make sense. Hunter was no threat to him. Hunter was just an innocent man who got a job at the wrong place. I bit my lower lip as I realized that nothing was coincidental in life. I'd learnt that from my time at the private club. Not only that, though. I was starting to wonder if Hunter was so innocent after all. Things weren't really adding up. The look in his eyes and the comments he'd made to me, didn't make sense. Part of me felt like he'd never really recognized me, though I didn't understand why he would lie. What was the point?

"Are you okay, Nancy?" Amber put her arm around my shoulder and gave me a sympathetic glance. "I know you loved him."

"I didn't love him." I stood there, still in shock, wanting to throw her arm off of my shoulder. "He was someone I had a crush on in high school."

"Yeah, he was your first love, right?" Amber continued. I knew at that point that she was trying to dig it in. She was trying to make it hurt more. She had no idea that I wasn't as soft as I appeared to be.

"What really is love?" I tilted my head and looked at her. "There are many types of love, aren't there? Self-love, love of money, love of fame, infatuation, lust, love of sex." I stopped then and looked her in the eyes. "I had a school girl crush on Hunter and yes, I'm sad about his death, but no, I didn't love him."

"I see." Her eyes narrowed and I could see her thinking. She wanted to hurt me and yet, I didn't know why. She'd seemed so open and friendly the first time I'd met her, but now, I could see that was all an act. She wasn't a nice person. She was jealous and vindictive. I just didn't know why.

"I hope Shannon is okay. She's the one who knew him better than me. He was her teacher, after all."

"Shannon's fine." Amber frowned and I saw her looking at Louise. I looked down and pretended that I hadn't seen the almost imperceptible shake of Louise's head. Something was going on here, something deeper and darker than I already knew. I just wasn't sure what. I followed them into the study and wondered if I was going to have to talk to the police and identify the body. I shuddered at the thought. I didn't want to do either. I just wanted to go home. I just wanted to go back to a time before I'd met all of these people. Though, that would also mean I'd have to forget meeting Jaxon. I wasn't sure how I felt about that. I was happy he was still alive. In fact, my heart soared at the thought. However, I felt confused and lost at my feelings. It wasn't like he was any sort of prince or savior. The door creaked as it opened and I froze. I knew exactly who was walking into the room. I could sense it in my body.

"You're here?" I whispered as I turned around and watched him walking through the door.

"I'm not sure if that makes you happy or sad." His familiar eyes searched mine and I shrugged nonchalantly, as if my heart hadn't leapt for joy at the sight of him.

"You're alive," I spoke again, not sure what to say.

"Hunter isn't." His eyes darkened as he studied my face. "Are you okay?"

"I'm fine." I swallowed hard, suddenly feeling uncomfortable at just how okay I felt.

"You came here for him." He spoke quietly. I knew that Louise and Amber were standing behind me trying to listen in to our conversation.

"I came here for you," I answered softly and he froze. I could tell that he hadn't expected that response. "Isn't that what you came to hear?"

"What about…" His voice trailed off and he looked away. I knew he was confused. Ultimately, I was confused as well. The whole thing seemed bigger than me.

"I meant to say, ultimately, it was you that sent me the invitation, not Hunter. So ultimately, it was because of you that I came to be here."

"I thought you were going to say something else." He ran his hands through his hair and closed his eyes for a few seconds. When he opened them again, his expression looked tired and I could see a bruise on his cheekbone.

"How did you…" I started to ask, and reached my hand up to his bruise. I stopped as I saw him flinch at my touch. I pulled my hand away and sighed. I wasn't sure if I wanted to know the answer to my unfinished question.

"Come with me." He grabbed my hand and I let him lead me out of the room and up the staircase. I knew I was making a mistake as I went with him. There were still too many unanswered questions, but I knew that in that moment I didn't care. I just needed to be with him. After the stress and worry of the last hour, I needed to just soak him in and memorize his every feature. I knew that I needed to leave the academy. This was no longer fun and games. This was serious. I was in over my head and I knew that I had to leave. Even if that meant saying goodbye to the one man I never wanted to forget. I knew that this was more than I'd signed up for.

***

"Where were you?" Jaxon pushed me into his bedroom.

"I went out for a walk."

"By yourself?"

"Who else would I be going with?"

"I don't know? Your dad, perhaps?"

"My dad?" I frowned at him. "What are you talking about?"

"I had a visit last night from your dad and his partner."

"Katie?"

"Katie?" He smiled and then laughed. "I wish Katie." His eyes lightened for a second and then he looked back at me. "I'm talking about Greyson."

"Oh." I bit my lower lip. Meg must have told them that something was going on. I should have known better than to confide in her. I knew she had my best interests at heart and wouldn't have said anything if she hadn't been worried, though I was still upset. "What did they want?"

"What do you think they wanted?" He sat on the bed and untied his shoes.

"I don't know. Where are they? Why didn't they try and take me home?" I frowned and thought for a moment. If they had really come to the academy, wouldn't I have been their first priority?

"They came to threaten me." He shrugged. "They came to tell me to leave you alone. I told them I wasn't the reason you came. Hunter was."

"Oh." My jaw dropped. "Why did you say that?"

"I wanted them to know the truth." He started unbuttoning his shirt. "You came because you're in love with Hunter and you want him to take your virginity. Or I should say wanted. When he was still alive."

"No, I didn't."

"You're telling me, that when you first arrived you didn't have thoughts or hopes of Hunter taking your virginity?"

"No." I paused. "I mean I had thoughts of us being together. Whatever that means. Kissing or hugging or whatever. But no, I didn't have dreams of having sex with him."

"So those dreams only started with me, then?"

"Yes, I mean, no." I was taken aback and flustered by his comment. "I've thought about it, yes, but only because..." My voice trailed off.

"Only because I'm a sex magnet that you can't resist." He threw his shirt on the ground and stood up. I watched as he undid his belt and pulled his pants down. He stood there in front of me in a pair of white boxers and white socks. I tried not to stare at his chest and then I tried to ignore the bulge in his boxers as well. I failed at both.

"What are you doing?" I glared at him and then stared at the bruise on his chest. "Why do you have bruises on your chest and on your cheek?"

"No reason."

"Did my dad do this to you?"

"Your dad was too busy with Hunter."

"What are you saying?" I walked towards him so I could look him in the eyes. "Are you saying my dad killed Hunter?"

"I'm saying, how well do you know your dad?"

"What do you mean by that?"

"You just met him recently, right?" He took a step towards me. "Maybe you don't know what happened with your mom as well as you think you do."

"I'm not talking about this with you."

"Maybe you need to realize that your dad is the wolf in all of this. Maybe you need to realize that he's the bad guy. Maybe my father and I are the ones that were done wrong. Maybe we're the ones that deserve retribution. Maybe your father will stop at nothing to ensure the truth doesn't come out."

"He's a good man."

"He's so good that he left you with your grandparents when your mother died. He's so good that you didn't even know he existed until recently. Think about it, Nancy. What do you really know about him?"

"I know that he's a good father."

"To Harry." He took another step towards me and touched my shoulder. "And you know why?"

"Why?" I whispered as I stared into his eyes, mesmerized by him. I felt as if he were hypnotizing me.

"Because he's obsessed with Katie."

"He loves her." I shook my head and took a step back, trying to break the spell he had over me.

"He loves her as you loved Hunter." He took another step towards me. "He's obsessed with her."

"No, he loves her. There's a difference."

"Do you want to know why he left last night, Nancy? Do you want to know why he left without taking you?"

I nodded silently.

"I told him I didn't care what he did, but he had to let you stay. He had to let me marry you. If he didn't, I told him, I would tell Katie everything."

"Everything about what?" I frowned, my heart beating.

"I don't know if you're ready to hear this." He grabbed my face and stared into my eyes. "I don't know if you can handle the truth."

"I can handle anything."

"Katie and I dated." His eyes bore into mine. "Three years ago. I had just moved to the city. I was twenty-two, she was slightly older. We hit it off."

"Because you randomly met her or because you planned it?"

"Is there really a difference?" His fingers fell to my trembling lips. "We met. We went on a few dates. Despite her being slightly older, we were a good fit. I liked her."

"I see." I tried to look away, suddenly feeling jealous.

"Don't get it wrong, Nancy. I didn't love her. I didn't want to marry her. I was attracted to her. I wanted to fuck her. Long and hard, like I want to fuck you."

"You're a pig." I took another step back and hit the wall. I tried to push him away as he stepped closer to me, but his solid muscular mass was too much for me to move. He then pressed into me and I could feel his cock hardening against my stomach.

"You're prettier than her," his lips whispered against mine. "I want you more than I wanted her."

"I don't care." I shrugged. "I don't want to know."

"Don't be jealous, Nancy. It's you I'm with now."

"I'm not jealous," I lied.

"I didn't want to be with Katie, and Brandon didn't want that either."

"What are you saying?"

"I'm saying there's a lot you don't know."

"Why do you want to marry me?" I struggled against him. "It makes no sense."

"I want to marry you so I can protect you and myself." He sighed. "Your dad killed Hunter because I told him you guys messed around. What if he finds out the truth? Will he kill me, too?"

"I don't believe he killed Hunter."

"He hit me in the face and then he got Greyson to hit me as well." His body shook. "I need you to trust me, Nancy. I've been nothing but honest with you. We have a connection. I see you're an innocent bystander, just like me. Your dad is bad news. Yes, my dad and I wanted to bring him down, but that's because he ruined us. All we have left is the academy. And we wanted to hurt him like he hurt us. Evil doesn't deserve to win. I can't help it that your father is the devil."

"Meg told me that Greyson used to call himself the devil," I mumbled as I stared at him. I didn't know what to think. I didn't know Brandon well. I didn't really understand why he'd just abandoned me. Yet, I didn't know Jaxon either. All I knew was that we were attracted to each other and he wanted revenge on my father. Would he have told me the truth if he was really a bad guy, though? Maybe he was being honest. If he was, that meant my dad was a really bad guy. I couldn't fathom why he would kill Hunter, but then I didn't really know him. I'd often thought about him and Katie when I lay in bed. He loved her so much, yet sometimes I thought about their story and it freaked me out. There was a thin line between obsession and love and I did sometimes wonder if my dad hadn't crossed it. I sighed as I looked into Jaxon's wide eyes. They looked so sincere and caring, yet, part of me was afraid of him. I was afraid that he was manipulating me. I really didn't know the truth or what had really happened. I didn't trust Jaxon even though my heart soared to be with him and touched by him. My biggest problem was deciding whether to pretend I did trust him and believe him. What would he do if I let him know how conflicted I was! If he had murdered Hunter, then I was in danger. In fact, my whole family could be in danger. And if he was telling the truth, if he was truly innocent, then he was in danger. I knew in my heart I would never forgive myself if something happened to him. I had to make a decision.

"Nancy, you're shivering." His fingers stroked the top of my head and I rested my head against his chest. "I'm going to take care of you. You'll be okay."

"How did you guys choose Amber and Shannon to join the academy?" I whispered against his chest casually.

"Why?" he asked softly, still stroking my hair.

"I was just curious."

"You'll have to ask my dad; I'm not really sure of the process for the other girls."

"What about Louise?"

"Louise?" He paused. "She's been here for years. It's her life. There's nothing she'd rather be doing."

"Oh. Does she recommend or know any of the girls?"

"Oh no. Louise has no family," he whispered against my head. "She has no one to recommend."

I felt my stomach sinking at his words. I knew he was lying and I knew that he knew he was lying. I couldn't trust Jaxon. I knew from the intonation in his voice that he was hiding something from me. Only I had no idea what it was. Jaxon finally stepped back and I pushed past him quickly.

"Where are you going?" Jaxon frowned at me as I walked to the door.

"I'm leaving."

"Leaving?" He frowned again and his expression looked closed off, so much so that I couldn't tell what he was thinking.

"I think my time here is done."

"Because Hunter died?"

"No," I said, shaking my head. "Because I don't know how he died or rather who murdered him."

"I don't think you want to know." His voice was terse and his expression pained.

"Was it you or was it my father?" I bit my lower lip.

"I can't let you leave, Nancy." He shook his head.

"Why not?" I knew that this was going to be the time that he took me to the side and showed me his true colors and why I was here, or he was going to tell me that he was falling for me. I waited in sweet anticipation to find out which one was going to happen.

"You haven't finished the course."

"What course?" My heart dropped in disappointment.

"I haven't finished teaching you everything you have to learn."

"I don't want to learn any more," I said, shaking my head. "Frankly, you're not that good of a teacher."

"What?" His eyes narrowed and he grabbed my hands and brought me into him. His chest felt hard against me and I looked up at him with unblinking eyes.

"Let go of me," I said firmly, ignoring the rapid beating of my heart.

"What?" His eyes flashed at me with an emotion I didn't recognize.

"Unhand me," I said sarcastically and his lips curled up.

"This isn't college, Nancy. This isn't English 101."

"Maybe you need to go back to school, then, as you don't seem to understand what 'let go of me' means."

"I understand what 'let go of me' means." His small smile faded. "I'm just not going to do it."

"Why not?"

"Because we haven't gotten what we want."

"And what's that?"

"To fuck."

"Oh." I gasped and tried to pull away from him. "That's not going to happen."

"It's not?" He tilted his head to the side and studied me. "Isn't that why you came to the Lovers' Academy?"

"No," I whispered and suddenly I felt sad. "I came for Hunter."

"Your father killed him." He dropped my arms and stepped back.

"What are you talking about?" My breath caught and I tried to see if he was lying. "I don't believe you. My dad wouldn't do that."

"Brandon and Greyson were here last night for one reason and one reason alone."

"No." I shook my head, not wanting to believe it.

"Yes. Your father had a gun." He continued, "He came to kill. It was either going to be me or Hunter. Then he found out that Hunter dragged you here for the wrong reasons."

"But it was you..." My voice trailed off and he turned around.

"You're not leaving, Nancy."

"You can't make me stay."

"I can make you do many things."

"Why would you do that?"

"Because I want to marry you." His eyes darkened as my stomach flipped.

"What are you talking about? Why do you keep saying that?"

"I want to marry you." His voice sounded anything but loving.

"I think I want to leave now." I walked towards the door and waited for him to run up and grab me. My fingers gripped into the handle and turned slowly. He didn't stop me as I walked out of the door and hurried to my room. I was almost to my door when I heard Amber and Shannon arguing at the bottom of the stairs.

"Can we leave yet?" Shannon muttered, her face screwed up and sulky. Nothing like her usual timid expression.

"We'll leave when I say we can leave," Amber replied tartly.

"What about Louise?" Shannon sounded annoyed. "I thought she got a call about that show off Broadway?"

"She did, but like you said it's off Broadway, not on."

"Does that really matter?"

"In our family it does." Amber's voice was stiff. "What's your problem anyway?"

"Barry called and he's missing me."

"You need to move on from that chump."

"He's the father of my son. I'm not just going to move on. They want me to come home."

"It's nearly done, Shannon. We'll be going home soon." Amber sighed and paused. "What was that noise?" Her voice rose and I stepped back as quickly and quietly as I could and made my way to my room. My heart was pounding and my face was burning at the fear of nearly being caught. What had I just heard? It didn't make sense. How could Shannon have a son if she was a virgin? It didn't make any sense to me. What was going on here? I walked over to my bed and sat down. I'd never been more confused in my life. Why had Jaxon asked me to marry him? Why would Shannon come to a lovers academy and pretend she was a virgin if she had a kid and why had Hunter been killed? It made no sense. Absolutely no sense at all.

CHAPTER THREE

Jaxon

The best way to deal with feelings of guilt is to occupy your mind and ignore them. Once guilt sets in, there is no way to remove it. It tells you that you've done something wrong and you know it. It tells you that if you could go back, you might make a different decision. Guilt can kill you slowly. It creeps up on you and takes over your brain. I'm not really one for guilt. I'm not a sociopath; I do know when I've done something wrong, but I find it doesn't help to feel guilty about it. What's done is done. You move on and do the best you can to forget about it.

I felt my heart drop when Nancy left the room. I knew that she hadn't believed everything I'd said. Though, I knew she had wanted to believe. She'd wanted to believe very badly. She liked me. Though, I wasn't even sure if she realized how much. I wasn't sure if she knew that the connection we had wasn't normal. She might be blaming it on the sexual chemistry we'd had. The sexual chemistry that was eating me up inside. My cock was still rock hard, even though she'd left the room an hour earlier. I wanted more than anything to be inside of her and I knew she wanted it too. Though, I couldn't think about that. Not yet. Not right now. I was playing too dangerous a game. If she called home now, it would all be over.

I hadn't wanted to let her go. I hadn't wanted to risk everything blowing up now. Yet, I'd known I had to. I had to let her go. I had to let her think she could trust me, to a certain degree. Nothing would progress past this point, if she didn't trust me. It didn't help that I had my own questions. I walked over to the door and banged it with my fists, resisting the urge to slam my fist through the window. I wanted to break something. I wanted to feel pain and see blood. I needed to be reminded of what a sick and dangerous game this was. I was about to hit the door again when I received a phone call.

"Jaxon." My dad's voice was cold as I answered the phone.

"Yes?" I said warily.

"How is part two going?"

"It's going."

"You're not weakening?"

"I'm not weakening."

"It's a pity about what happened to Hunter." His voice held a question, but I didn't respond right away.

"Yes, it's a pity."

"Death is only the beginning."

"Yes."

"She's not a stupid girl."

"I know that."

"She'll start asking questions."

"She's already asking questions."

"Does she know anything?"

"Nothing more than we want her to know."

"You know what'll happen to her if this doesn't work."

"I know."

"Brandon won't be happy once he knows the truth."

"I know, Dad." My voice was annoyed.

"You don't have long."

"He thinks she's pregnant."

"Smart move." He paused and I could almost see the smile on his face. "The marriage will proceed, then."

"Of course it will." My voice was irritated. "She wants me. She wants to protect me. It will proceed."

"You've got a lot of faith in your answer."

"I've got a lot of faith in the way she reacts when I touch her."

"That's my boy." He laughed. "Enjoy the spoils while you can."

"It's not like that." My voice was stiff and I frowned at the empty space in front of me.

"Just make sure that you marry her before she finds out about the academy."

"She's not going to find out, Dad."

"Trust me, nothing stays a secret for long. She'll find out. And once she realizes that the Lovers' Academy doesn't really exist, she's going to ask questions. She's going to ask questions that neither of us is going to want to answer."

"She won't find out."

"Remember the rules of Chess I taught you when you were a boy. If you want to be a winner in the game, you must never start with the same openings. You must never count on one strategy for too long. Also, never underestimate your opponent. You must account for their accounting of your next ten moves. Figure out your strategy based on them figuring out your strategy, it is only then you can win the game."

"Winning the game doesn't always mean you're a winner, Dad."

"Winning this game is all that matters, Jaxon. Don't forget that. In a game of cat and mouse, the winner is the one who gets the cheese and survives, not just the one who gets to keep his life." And with that he hung up.

CHAPTER FOUR

Nancy

I woke up the next morning with a heavy head. I hadn't slept well and I didn't know what to do. I had nowhere to go. No one to talk to. I had no options. It scared me to feel so alone. I'd gone from having a loving family to nothing in a week. I felt isolated and unsure of myself. I knew I should just go back to Brandon's, wait out the summer and then go to college. That's what any normal person would do, but I wasn't normal.

BANG BANG. The knock on the door made me jump. I got out of bed slowly and walked over to the door, not sure who was waiting for me.

"Oh, it's you." I stared at Jaxon's calm, yet serious face.

"Yes, it's me. Can I come in?" He stood there patiently and I frowned at him.

"This is a bit out of the ordinary for you, isn't it? Since when do you knock?"

"Since I realized that you would prefer me to knock before I entered the room."

"It didn't seem to bother you before."

"Maybe not, but you didn't know how good masturbating felt before."

"Oh." I blushed up at him.

"I wouldn't want to catch you in the act." He grinned and walked into my room. "I might just have to finish you off myself."

"What's that supposed to mean?" I closed the door behind him and turned around.

"Well, it means, I can use my fingers or my cock. Though, this time, I think I'd much rather use my cock."

"You're…" I started, but he cut me off.

"Yes, I am." He grinned. "Whatever you were going to say is true. I am everything you think I am, including a good lover."

"Whatever."

"Don't tell me you haven't thought about it?"

"I haven't thought about it," I lied, trying to ignore the thoughts I'd had earlier this morning.

"Liar." He licked his lips.

"What do you want?"

"I wanted to make sure you were okay. Last night was crazy and I suspect today will be even crazier."

"Why? Another death?"

"I hope not." He shivered. "I'm talking about the police. They will want to question you this morning. They understood you were in shock last night, but I don't think they'll let it go another day."

"Why do they want to question me?"

"To see if you did it, of course." His eyes narrowed as he looked at me. "You didn't of course."

"Is that a question or a statement?" I looked into his eyes and frowned. "Because for a second there, it really sounded like a question."

"I think none of us can really know what happened until the police figure it out."

"I'm shocked you let the police come to investigate." I walked over to my bed and sat down and looked at him. "It seems to me that there are things that you and your father wouldn't want to get out."

"We're happy for the truth to come out. We don't evade the truth. We just want all the answers out in the open." He came and sat next to me. "How are you feeling this morning?" He stared into my face, his eyes a mere inch from my own.

"I'm fine." I shuffled away from him.

"You look like shit."

"Well, I didn't have the best sleep I've ever had in my life." I rolled my eyes. "Someone died here last night. I don't know why. I don't know who killed him. All I know is that he had my name on a piece of paper when he died."

"So who are your main suspects?"

"I'm not Sherlock Holmes. Or Olivia Benson." I smiled to myself as I thought of *Law and Order: SVU*. It always made me think of Meg.

"If you were, who would you suspect?" His voice was low as if he didn't care about my answer, but I knew that he did.

"You," I said directly and stared into his eyes. "You're my first suspect. Then my dad," I said reluctantly. "Then Amber."

"Amber." He looked confused. "The other student, Amber?"

"Yeah," I said, nodding. "There's something not right about that girl."

"Oh, why's that?"

"A good detective never tells her secrets."

"Why am I a subject?"

"Because I don't trust you."

"I see." I could see him studying my face. "You let me into your room, though."

"I let you in because better the devil you know then the devil you don't."

"So you think I'm a devil?" He smirked at me.

"Aren't you?"

"I'm not in hell." He shrugged. "Yet."

"You think this is all fun and games?"

"I don't think it's all fun, no." He shook his head. "Not yet."

"What do you want, Jaxon?"

"I want you on the bed, stomach down, ass in the air and begging me to enter you."

"Puh-lease." I rolled my eyes at him, though my body was shaking at his words.

"There's the eighteen-year-old in you." He shook his head and groaned.

"What's that supposed to mean?"

"Puh-lease." He imitated my voice and I couldn't stop myself from smiling.

"You think you're funny?"

"No, I think I'm horny."

"Is this all about sex for you?"

"This is the Lovers' Academy." He touched my face. "I'm your teacher."

"Okay."

"Are you ready for your lesson today?"

"What's the lesson?" I asked slowly, not believing that I was even entertaining the idea.

"Some more rope play."

"Rope play?" I repeated, confused. "What does that mean?"

"It means I want to show you how to have fun with ropes."

"Fun with ropes? How?"

"I want to use this rope." He held up a piece of rope. I had no idea where it came from.

"Around my wrists?"

"No, around your neck." His face was grim. "I won't hurt you."

"Are you fucking joking?" I started laughing, partly due to shock. "There is no way in hell you're using that rope around my neck."

"Why?" His lips twitched and his eyes changed from a serious glare to a surprised one.

"Did you seriously think I was just going to say yes to that?" I gave him a crazy look. "Did you think I would say, 'Sure Jaxon, tie a rope around my neck and let's have some fun'?"

"I guess not." He laughed. "We can use it in other ways."

"Maybe I can tie you up this time." I smiled sweetly. "If we're doing this whole trust thing."

"You want to tie me up?" His eyes narrowed.

"Yes." I moved closer to him and pushed him down onto the bed. "I want to tie you up." I let my inner seductress come out as I stared at him. "I want to see how much you can take."

"How much what?" He grabbed my wrists.

"How much anything? You're not the only one who can be a tease."

"You want to tease me?"

"I want to see if I can trust you."

"And teasing me will let you know if you can trust me?"

"No, you letting me tie you up with rope will let me know if you trust me."

"I trust you." He rolled over and pushed me down onto the bed. "I trust you or I wouldn't be here. I wouldn't have told you about my dad and your dad. I wouldn't have suggested we get married."

"About that." I squirmed against him. "It doesn't make sense to me that you want to get married. Why would you want to get married?"

"I want both of us to be safe. I feel like the only way both of us will be safe from our fathers is by being together."

"Hmm." I sighed as I looked up at him. I wanted to believe him so badly. I wanted him to be genuine. I wanted him to really be concerned with protecting me. I wanted to be number one in someone's life for once.

"It's the only way, Nancy." He kissed my forehead. "We can take care of each other."

"You're the one that started this."

"I didn't know your dad would become a murderer."

"I'm not so sure my dad is a murderer." I shook my head.

"Did you call him?" His eyes were intense and I shook my head.

"No," I whispered. "Not yet. I needed time to think."

"Think about what?"

"I don't want to talk about this right now." I sighed and shifted under him. "I didn't know that therapy was a part of the lesson."

"It's only a part if you want it to be a part."

"I don't want it to be a part." I shook my head.

"Then we don't talk."

"That's what you guys prefer, right?" I tried to ignore the touch of his fingers on my breast. "You prefer it when the girl doesn't want to talk."

"Depends on the girl and the conversation." His fingers found my nipple. "I don't mind talking when it's something I want to hear."

"Or if it's something you want to touch, right?" My hand crept up to his. "Then you pretend to listen."

"I don't pretend to do anything." He growled and moved his mouth down to my breast. "I just do." His lips bit down on my breast and he sucked on my nipple through my top.

"Jaxon, no."

"No?" He frowned. "What do you mean no?"

"I mean, no, I'm not doing this now." I pushed him away and jumped off of the bed. "You can't just come into my room with a rope and ask me to do kinky shit and think I'm just going to say yes."

"You're a typical girl."

"What does that mean?"

"Your body says one thing, your mouth says another."

"Are you out of your fucking mind?" I glared at him as I shouted. "Do you think that's cool or funny?"

"Do I think what's cool?" He jumped up and glared back at me. "Having blue balls every damn night?"

"Women's bodies respond in ways we can't control," I snapped. "Do you think you have the right to do anything to a woman's body based on what her body is telling you, or do you think you should listen to what she's saying?"

"You really think I'm a jerk, don't you?"

"I don't know what to think. I don't know you."

"What's going on here, Nancy?" He sighed and sat back down on my bed. "Are you mad at me?"

"I've nothing to be mad at you about." I shook my head and turned around. My head felt like it was spinning. I was confused and unsure of everything that was going on around me. I just wanted to go back to bed so that I could fall asleep and forget everything that had happened the last couple of weeks. I just wanted to ignore the fact that my nipple was still aching and tingling for his touch. I wanted to ignore the fact that I wanted to touch Jaxon and taste him. I wanted to tease him until he couldn't take it anymore. I wanted him to want me so badly that my very touch would make him blow.

"I'm going to go to my room." He walked towards the door. "I see you need time to think and be by yourself."

"You're leaving me by myself?"

"Yes," he said, nodding. "You need to have a clear head. Obviously, it's not clear right now. I'm not going to do anything with you until your head is clear."

"I don't know what to say." I bit my lip, feeling shocked that he was leaving so early. Had I annoyed him? Was he no longer interested in me? I was angry at myself for feeling so weak. Already I was starting to doubt what I'd said to him and how I'd acted. Maybe I should go with what my body was feeling, instead of the indecision in my brain. I was about to ask him to stay when he walked out of the door. I closed my eyes and stood there wondering what I was going to do. I froze as it suddenly hit me that Hunter was dead. I'm not sure why the reaction was so delayed, but I stood there in the middle of my room with tears streaming down my face and all I could think was I'd gotten Hunter killed. I'd gotten him killed and I didn't even know who was responsible for his death.

CHAPTER FIVE

Jaxon

Timing is crucial in every aspect of life. When you meet the love of your life, the time makes a difference. For example, if you meet them in grade school or junior high, that's bad timing. If you meet them in college, that's perfect timing. Timing in investments is also key: buy low, sell high. Everything in life revolves around timing. Success revolves around timing. My timing with Nancy could make or break everything.

There's one thing you can't account for in timing and that's emotions. Emotions can ruin everything. I've never had to worry about that before. In fact, I've never wanted to care about anyone else before. Love was a weakness I couldn't afford in life. Not after everything that had happened. Even though I knew that, I was finding it hard to feel impartial about Nancy. She was everything I didn't want her to be. Honest, beautiful, charming, trusting, sexy, beautiful. She had an air about her that was fragile. She was broken inside. I could see that. I could see that and I was playing on it. My father would have been proud. Everything he'd ever taught me was based around the fact that I should be able to read people. When you can read people you can figure out answers to questions you didn't even have to ask.

I loved knowing people's fears and loves and playing them against them. Sometimes it's easy and sometimes it's hard. Especially when they have a good poker face. Brandon had a good poker face. I hadn't even known about Katie until I'd come across an article about a museum event they'd been photographed at. They weren't even standing together in the photo, but I'd seen the way he was looking at her. He loved her. He loved her more than he loved himself. She was to be my *in.* And it had worked. Even though they'd been broken up for years, Brandon had still showed up at my doorstep warning me to stay away from her. He'd had no idea who I was. If he had, I was positive that he wouldn't have given me all the ammunition he had. However, I'd been the one to come out ahead. I'd told him that Katie and I were getting serious. I'd told him that we were thinking about taking it to the next level. It had all been a lie, of course. Katie hadn't been interested in me in that way, but he didn't know that. Even now, he thought that he'd busted up a serious relationship with his stalking. I knew that I was close to him finding out the truth. I had to get Nancy to marry me, before all the lies came pouring out.

I quickly pulled out my phone and called Brandon. It was a call I didn't want to make yet, but it was a call I had to make.

"Brandon Hastings."

"It's Jaxon Cade."

"What do you want?" His voice lowered and I could tell he was pissed. I smiled to myself at his tone. He was going to become even more pissed once I was done with him.

"She said she wants to marry me. She wants her child to know his father." I lied smoothly, the words flowing from my mouth as if they were water flowing from a stream.

"So this is how this is going to go, then? You're going to marry my daughter?"

"Better than your fiancée, right? Though I'm sure Katie would like to know the real story of why we broke up."

"If Nancy wants to marry you." He sighed. "I don't think it's a good idea."

"We're in love."

"She barely knows you."

"You know what it's like when you're young. You fall in love quickly. And now we're having a child. Well, you know how it is. Now that we're having a child, everything in our relationship seems bigger and brighter."

"You're lucky I don't kill you for sleeping with my daughter."

"You don't want more blood on your hands, do you?" I was about to ask him about Hunter when I heard a knock on my door. "Hold on." I walked to the door and opened it. "Hey." I frowned and pulled her into the room quickly. "You shouldn't be here," I whispered.

"I needed to see you," she whispered back.

"I have to go now, Brandon, or should I say Dad." I laughed into the phone and hung up.

"Who were you talking to?" Amber pressed her lips against mine and I pulled away.

"I told you, no kissing."

"I don't understand why you don't kiss." She sighed and pulled off her top. "It's so impersonal."

"You knew this from the beginning."

"Doesn't mean I like it." She pulled her bra off and I stared at her breasts in a clinical fashion. "I was surprised to get your text."

"I was horny." I shrugged. "You should have waited to come until tonight. What if someone had seen you?"

"Who's going to see me?" She dropped to the ground and undid my zipper.

"Anyone." I frowned down at her as she pulled my cock out. "I don't want anyone knowing that we know each other."

"You mean intimately?" She giggled before putting my cock into her mouth. She got to work immediately, sucking me off and playing with my balls. She knew exactly what I liked and she did it well. Though all I could think about was what my next step would be with Nancy. She was getting to me in ways I never thought possible. She was complicating everything. I was so close to accomplishing everything I'd ever dreamed of. So close. Yet, something was holding me back. If I was honest with myself, I knew it wasn't something, it was someone. Amber continued sucking on my cock and I knew that I was about to blow my load. I didn't bother pulling out or warning Amber that I was about to come. I knew she didn't love swallowing, but I didn't care. I'd been fucking her on and off for the last year. I had absolutely no concern for her, but I was happy that she was eager to please. If it hadn't been for her, I wouldn't have had Shannon and Louise here, playing their roles.

I came hard and fast, my cock exploding in her mouth. Her eyes widened as she continued sucking and swallowing. She stood up after a few minutes, licking her lips and playing with her nipples.

"My turn now." She smiled at me. "I need to feel your tongue inside of me."

"I'm afraid that's not going to be possible." I dismissed her, staring at her body in disdain. I had no interest in touching her. All I could think about was Nancy. I was starting to feel angry at myself. What the fuck was going on here?

"What do you mean that's not possible?" She slipped her fingers into her panties. "I'm fucking wet." She pulled out her fingers and ran them across my now-limp cock. "Feel that? I'm soaking. I need to feel you inside of me."

"I'm going to have to ask you to leave." My eyes narrowed. "Now."

"I thought you were horny?"

"I was. I've come now." I nodded and gave her a short smile. "Thanks."

"Bastard." She shook her head. "This is all a game to you, isn't it?"

"You know it's never going to be more than that."

"I know that." She shrugged and grabbed her top off of the floor. "Does your little girl, Nancy, know that, though?" She pulled her top on. "I'd hate to think she believes the bullshit you're spewing in her ear."

"Is that a threat?" I grabbed her wrists. "You're not planning on saying anything, are you?"

"I don't care either way." She pulled her wrists away from me. "You're the one who has to pretend you're interested in her. I think it's stupid, but you have your reasons."

"I'm not pretending," I answered softly and I saw her eyes widening in shock. I couldn't blame her. She knew me as the cold, heartless man that I was. There had been many nights when all we'd done was her sucking my cock and then I'd dismiss her. She'd never stayed the night. We'd never kissed. I didn't care if she had an orgasm when I fucked her. The fact was I didn't care about her. She was just one in a long line of women I used at my disposal. She was one of a long line of women I didn't give a fuck about. All that was starting to change, though. I was starting to have feelings. I did kiss now. I did care about a women coming more than myself. Of course, the one person I would start to have feelings for happened to be the one person I was going to bring down. "You can leave now. Don't come to my room again."

"You're the one that…" She started and stopped when she saw my look.

"If you tell Nancy anything, you'll be cut off."

"I know. I'm sorry. I'm just trying to help."

"So far you guys have been great." I nodded. "Just keep it up."

"Shannon wants to know when she can leave. Her boyfriend is starting to wonder where she is. And she misses her son."

"Soon." I turned away from her. "She'll be able to leave soon."

"Okay." I could see from Amber's expression that she wanted to ask what happened next. I knew what she wanted, even if she didn't want to admit it. I knew she wanted me. I could see it in her face and the way she stared at me when she thought no one was looking. I'd have to get rid of her after I married Nancy. In fact, I was happy to get rid of her. Though I had my reasons for marrying Nancy, I knew I'd very much enjoy the intimate parts of our relationship. I just had to ensure that she said yes. Everything depended on her marrying me. I tried to ignore the fact that my heart was also excited. That was the last part of my body that I needed to feel excited about marrying Nancy. I'd cut my heart out of my chest myself, if I thought it was going to ruin my plan. I'd come too far to let anything get in the way. I was so close to victory I could taste it.

CHAPTER SIX

Nancy

It was hard not to stop feeling guilty about Hunter. I kept waiting for the police to question me, but no knock ever came on my door. I was surprised that Jaxon didn't appear at the door either. A part of me wondered if he was done with me. Maybe he was trying to figure out how he could expel me from the academy and still keep part of us safe.

Part of me thought I should leave, but I wasn't sure where to go. I wasn't 100% sure that my father wasn't involved in Hunter's death and that made me sad. The other part of me was scared and upset that I didn't trust my father 100%. I could barely believe that I had doubts about him already, but I knew that was only natural. I didn't even really know him. I knew him better than Jaxon, but barely.

I decided to go for a walk to make myself feel better and to try and stop thinking about Jaxon and his suggestions. I was almost scared to go for a walk around the grounds after what had happened last time, but I figured it was the only thing that could keep me sane right now. I left the house quickly, not wanting to be seen by anyone. It was only when I got outside that I saw Shannon and Louise talking at the side of the building by one of the tall oak trees. I knew that I wanted to hear what they were saying. I kept my head down and walked slowly to the side of the house, making sure to stay as close as I could to the building.

"I don't know what she sees in him." Louise sounded annoyed. "If I miss this audition, I'm going to be pissed." Louise sounded very different from her normal demeanor.

"You know Amber, she always chooses the wrong guys." Shannon shrugged. "At least we're making good money."

"Yeah, ten grand will keep me for a few months, but man, I'm over it. Jaxon needs to hurry this shit up."

"Amber said that it was nearly all complete." Shannon shrugged. "Supposedly she spoke to him."

"Good, this place gives me the creeps and his father too."

"Oh shit, didn't you know? That's not his dad."

"What?" Louise's voice sounded as shocked as I felt.

"That's not his dad. That old man is his..." Shannon's voice died as we all heard a large twig snap. "What the fuck was that?" she exclaimed and Louise looked around with a scared expression.

"I'm telling you, Shannon, this place is creepy. Amber might be my cousin, but I'm out of here if things don't start looking kosher soon. This place is giving me the creeps."

"I know." Shannon sighed. "It was those two guys that came the other night that have me freaked out. One of them had a gun. I'm not joking. Jaxon is playing with fire. I don't wanna get stuck here when the house burns down. You know, metaphorically. Or figuratively." She frowned. "Or is it literally? Maybe not literally." She sighed. "You know what I mean?"

"Yup, I know." Louise's voice was still loud. "It's time for us to get out of Dodge."

"Yeah, I mean, that Nancy had better take his offer before things go crazy."

"I know, I can't believe that..."

Another twig snapping made us all jump. I knew that I had to get away quickly before they saw me. I tiptoed back to the front door and went inside the house. All thoughts of me going on a walk vanished from my mind. What the hell was going on here? My heart was pounding. Could Shannon have been telling the truth that the old man wasn't Jaxon's father? It didn't seem possible to me. I'd witnessed private conversations that led me to believe that he was Jaxon's dad. Why make that up? Why tell me a story about his dad wanting revenge on me if it wasn't even his dad? It didn't make sense. For a second I wondered if maybe the revenge had something to do with Katie. Was Jaxon in love with her? Did Jaxon want to try and win her back? It made no sense to me. He didn't seem to be in love with anyone. And I didn't think he was delusional. He couldn't be doing all this to get Katie back, could he? It just didn't make any sense. And I didn't understand why he had lied about knowing Amber and the other girls. They obviously weren't here for the classes. Even though they had said they were at the train station. They hadn't acknowledged knowing Louise either when we'd arrived, which meant that they had been lying from the beginning. Just like Jaxon and his 'maybe' dad. My heart started pounding as I realized that they had to have been in on it from the beginning as well. This had all been a set-up. I tried to remember what Amber and Shannon had said to me the first time I'd met them, but I couldn't. I couldn't remember. I felt so frustrated and annoyed at myself as I walked up the stairs. It was weird how used to the house I'd gotten. Almost as if it were my home. I laughed at the irony of the matter. As if this creepy old house could ever be my home. I walked quickly to my room. The room that had become my safe haven. I knew there was only one thing for me to do. I needed to call Meg and I needed to get out of here. I was in over my head and as much as I wasn't sure if I trusted my dad, I did trust Meg.

I rushed to my bed and pulled my bag out from underneath it. I unzipped the bag and attempted to pull out my phone. I could feel my heart racing as I realized the phone wasn't there. I swallowed hard as I dumped the contents of my bag into the bed. It still wasn't there.

"Fuck it," I muttered under my breath. Where was my phone?

"Everything okay?" Jaxon's voice boomed as he entered my room.

"You didn't knock." I turned around quickly. My face was red and I was angry. "I thought you were going to from now on."

"Sorry, I thought you didn't care."

"Of course I care." I glared at him. "I don't want you to just keep coming in my room without my permission."

"What's happened to you, Nancy?" He walked over to me and frowned. "You seem tense."

"You think?" I glared at him again, wanting to hit him against the chest hard and repeatedly. How could he do this to me? Why was it that whenever he appeared I felt my resolves weaken? There was something about his presence that made me doubt myself and my feelings. There was something about him that made me want to give him a second chance.

"What are you looking for?" He stared at the contents of my bag on my bed with narrowed eyes.

"My pills," I said sarcastically. He knew what I was looking for. I was pretty sure he was the one who had taken my phone.

"What pills?" he asked in a concerned voice and I looked at his face to see if he was lying. As I stared at him I knew that I had absolutely no clue if he was being honest or not.

"Forget about it." I shrugged. "It doesn't matter."

"What's wrong, Nancy?" He grabbed my shoulders and turned me to face him.

"Nothing," I muttered and then looked up into his eyes. "Unless you want to start telling me the truth about what's really going on here?"

"Nancy," he said, looking around the room slowly. "You need to be calm." He whispered in my ear, "I'm going to tell you everything, but I need to make sure there are no bugs in your room." He put his finger to his mouth and walked around the room checking every possible spot to see if there were any bugs. I stared at him in shock and fear. Had someone been listening to us this whole time? I shivered as I thought of the other possibility. Had someone been watching us? My eyes widened as I looked up to the ceiling to see if there were any cameras.

"They wouldn't put cameras in." Jaxon saw my face and walked up to me. "And it looks as if we're bug-free."

"How do you know?"

"I've put in a whole lot of bugs in my time." He shrugged. "Anyway, Nancy. You need to listen to me and listen to me good. I'm not sure I'm going to be able to say this more than once. It pains me to say this as I don't want to betray my father, but I think he hired Amber, Louise and Shannon to work here so that he could spy on us. There's something I haven't told you. I know Amber from the past. She and I used to hook up. I know I should have told you before, but I really didn't know how to. I was shocked when I saw her arrive at the house. I was shocked to find out recently that she knows Louise and Shannon. Nancy, I think my father had Hunter killed. He hated that Hunter wasn't going along with his plan. I think we need to get married because it is the one thing I can do to protect you. I really feel like he's coming after you. And I really feel like Brandon is coming after me. I feel that the only way we can be truly safe is if we are married. Neither one of them will try anything then. They both love us more than they hate the other one. If we get married and convince them that it's real, I think we have a fighting shot at living a normal life. It doesn't have to be for forever. Maybe just a year or two. I know this is my fault. I instigated everything, but I had no idea that it would go this far. I didn't know what my dad was capable of. I didn't know he had so much hate in his heart for your father."

I stared into Jaxon's wide eyes and all I could think about was what perfect lips he had. Everything else had me in shock, I didn't even know how to respond. What could I say to everything? How could I pretend to even understand everything he was saying? If anything, he'd only made me more confused.

"I heard Shannon telling Louise that your father wasn't your father." I bit my lower lip and stared into his eyes.

"Nancy." He touched my face and leaned forward to kiss me. "Of course he's my father. Who else would he be? They're playing a game with you, Nancy. I'm sure they even knew you were standing there listening. Don't you get it, Nancy? They want to turn us against each other. Do you know that Amber told me that she was suspicious of the fact that you were on a walk when Hunter was killed? She wanted me to think that you were in on it. She wanted me to think that you called your dad. She wanted me to think that you're the one who set it up so that he beat me up and brought a gun."

"I didn't do that, Jaxon. I swear." My eyes bulged open and I touched his jaw. "I haven't spoken to my dad since I've been here." I gasped. "I don't know why she would think that?"

"She's obviously working for my dad. They are trying to destroy our trust of each other, but that's all we have left now, Nancy. All we have is each other. My father used me. He wanted me to do anything to bring you down, but I couldn't." His voice broke as he spoke. "Once I got to know you, I realized that I couldn't be the one to do this to you and your family. Yes, I hate your dad for what he did to my family, but, well, I kind of like you, Nancy. You've made me realize that I'm more than who I thought I was. You've made me realize that revenge isn't always the answer. You're special to me, Nancy. You've trusted me and given me reason to believe that I can have a life outside of this. I don't know what this marriage will be like. I can't even guarantee that it's the right step for us. I don't really do love. I'm not hardwired that way, but what I do know is that when I'm with you something feels different. I'm different. I want to be a better man. That sounds cliché, doesn't it?" He sighed. "I'm not even sure what I'm saying anymore. I'm just trying to tell you that I'm a different man right now. I'm different from the man that sent you those invitations."

"Why?" I whispered, feeling my heart pounding. "Why are you different?"

"I wish I could explain it." He shrugged. "All I know is that I think differently now. I don't want you to get hurt." His face looked pained and he ran his fingers down my cheek. "I'd kill myself if anything ever happened to you."

"I think this is the most honest you've ever been." I spoke thoughtfully, staring at his eyes. They seemed to burn bright with the truth.

"I do believe that it is." His fingers ran down my neck and he kissed me on the lips and then moved back. "You don't know how big this is for me."

"What?"

"Nothing." He sighed and then kissed my neck. "It doesn't matter." He bit down on my neck and kissed hard. "I love the taste of you." He groaned and licked across my collarbone. "I want to be with you so badly."

"I want you too," I whispered.

"What?" He pulled back and stared at me. "What are you saying?"

"I'm saying that I want to make love to you." I smiled. "Or rather, I want you to make love to me."

"Are you sure?" he asked softly and stroked my hair.

"Yes." I nodded.

"As a teacher or…" His voice trailed off.

"I want you to make love to me as a man who wants to be with me, not as a teacher."

"You don't want me to be your teacher anymore?"

"I don't know." I grinned. "Right now, I want you to be my teacher and so much more."

"You're going to give me whiplash, you know. I can't even keep up with you." He laughed as he picked me up. "I just want to be all you hoped for."

"I'm sure you will be." I giggled, suddenly feeling light-headed. "Thank you for being honest with me." I stroked his face. "I know how confusing this whole situation is as I'm just as confused as you are. I want to hate you and run away, but I just can't. There's something between us. I don't know what it is. Maybe we're kindred spirits."

"Yes, maybe that's what it is." He nodded and plopped me down on the bed. "We're kindred spirits that are about to become lovers."

"Do you have protection?" I looked up at him and smiled. "I don't want us to have to stop because you have to find some."

"Has that happened to you before, then?" He raised an eyebrow at me.

"No." I shook my head.

"I always have protection on me." He pulled a silver packet out of his pocket. "You never know when you're going to get lucky."

"I don't know how I feel about that." I pursed my lips and then frowned as I remembered something he'd said. "So you and Amber?" I bit my lower lip and paused.

"What about us?" He pulled my top off and then undid my bra. I lay there thinking as he buried his face in my breasts.

"Did you guys have sex?"

"Do you really want to know?" He flicked my nipple with his tongue and I groaned as he bit down on my tender bud.

"Yes." I moaned and then groaned as his fingers played with my other breast. "I don't know." I moaned as his lips switched to my other breast and he sucked hard.

"You don't want to know. Trust me," he muttered between sucks. "She and I haven't been intimate in months. She means nothing to me."

"She's into you." I wiggled on the bed underneath him and sighed as I thought about Amber's comments about Jaxon and his cock. She hadn't just been making idle talk. She'd known exactly what she was saying.

"Forget her, she's not important."

"Have you been with anyone else here before?" I sighed. "And why would your father hire them to come to the academy?"

"I told you, he wanted you to become friends with them, so he could spy on you. He wanted to know everything you're thinking and doing. It's how he's been able to keep one step ahead of us, until right now. He can't do that now because we're one step ahead of him. If we get married, we'll ruin his plans and we'll protect ourselves from the wrath of both of our fathers."

"Oh, Jaxon." I moaned as he pulled my pants down in one fell swoop along with my panties. His face moved down from my breasts quickly and I felt his tongue in-between my legs, licking me eagerly. "Oh, my," I cried out in ecstasy. "Don't stop." I moaned and scratched his back as he sucked on my clit and nibbled it gently. I could feel my pussy shivering against his lips. I was so horny, I wasn't even sure I was making sense.

"I won't stop." He grunted. "But let's stop talking about Amber and our fathers now, please. This is our time. Let's make sure we both enjoy it and make the most of it."

"Okay." I moaned and closed my eyes. All I could think about was his lips on me, his tongue inside of me and his teeth teasing me. It was almost too much. The pleasure and the anticipation of an orgasm were killing me.

"Come for me, Nancy." He groaned as he pushed his tongue in and out of me. I imagined it was his cock and I felt my pussy lips quivering. His tongue felt so good inside of me. He increased the pace of his tongue movements and then I felt his lips sucking down on my clit, hard. I came fast and furiously, my wetness going all over his face. Jaxon groaned against my pussy and I felt his tongue licking me up eagerly. "You taste so sweet, Nancy." He groaned and jumped up. I watched him pulling his shirt off and then pulling his jeans down. He wasn't wearing boxers and I stared at his hard cock in amazement as he got back down on the bed and moved on top of me.

"We're going to do it missionary style?" I looked at him in surprise and he laughed.

"You really think I'm the kink master, don't you?"

"I'm just surprised." I pulled him down towards me. "You didn't seem a missionary type of man."

"I'm not." He nodded in agreement. "But for your first time, I wanted it to be sweet and gentle. I also wanted to make sure that I watched your face the first time you felt a cock inside of you."

"You don't have to be sweet and gentle." I shook my head. "I can't see that the rope man is sweet and gentle in bed."

"The rope man?" He smiled and leaned down and kissed me. I could feel his hardness pressed against me. "I like that."

"You seem to like to do a lot of kinky shit with rope."

"I like to do a lot of kinky shit, period." He winked at me and I felt his chest pressed down into my breasts. I wrapped my legs around his waist and he groaned. "But I'm glad you appreciate the rope."

"I do appreciate the rope," I answered, slightly embarrassed to admit it. "It really seems to heighten the experience."

"It does. We'll use that and other toys later. Today is just about the experience. I want your first time to be amazing just for it being your first time." He stroked my face and moved my legs with his hands. "I want you to remember how you felt when you first felt the tip of my cock against your wet pussy." He moved his cock against my pussy and rubbed gently. "I want you to remember how you felt when you felt the tip of me against your clit." He rubbed my clit aggressively and I cried out.

"Please, Jaxon." I shifted on the bed. "I can't take much more of this."

"I want you to remember the first time I entered you." He guided his cock to my entrance and pushed in slowly. "Look at me." He stared down into my eyes and smiled as I gasped loudly. His cock was slow and deliberate as he entered me and I wasn't sure if he was going to fit inside of me.

"How big are you?" I moaned as he continued his entry inside of me.

"You'll have to measure me sometime." He winked at me and then thrust hard.

"Oooh," I screamed as I felt a sharp jab of pain.

"It won't hurt for long," he whispered against my lips and then started moving slowly in and out of me. He was right, within seconds the pain had turned to exquisite pleasure. I started moving my hips back and forth on the bed to match his movements. His cock felt so hard and delicious inside of me.

"Oh, shit." He groaned as he pulled out of me quickly.

"What are you doing?" I cried out as his cock left me.

"I need to put a rubber on. Hold on." He jumped up and I watched as he quickly slid a condom on his hard cock.

"Oh my God, Jaxon." I screamed as he entered me again. This time there was nothing gentle about his movements. He moved in and out of me quickly and his breathing also increased as he got into it. He pulled my legs up and placed them over his shoulders and I screamed as he entered me. I felt him harder and deeper than before and I understood in that moment exactly why people were so addicted to sex. This was the best feeling in the world. I'd never felt so high before in my life. I felt like I was flying, soaring through the sky. I never knew that my body could experience such pleasure.

"I'm about to come, Nancy," he whispered against my lips. "Come for me." His fingers reached down and rubbed my clit as he continued fucking me and I came hard and fast. That seemed to please him because he grinned before stilling. I felt his cock slowing as he came. His body jerked for a few seconds and then he collapsed on top of me and kissed me hard. I kissed him equally as hard back, not thinking about anything other than what had just happened and how great it had made me feel.

"I'll marry you," I whispered to Jaxon. "If it's going to help both of us and we can have more moments like this, then yes, I'll marry you." I smiled up at him and rested my head against his chest. "I'll marry you whenever you want."

CHAPTER SEVEN

Jaxon

"I should win a fucking Academy Award." I muttered into the phone. "It's done."

"Good," he replied. "Congratulations."

"Don't sound so happy for me," I said sarcastically and growled, angry that he didn't sound as happy as I thought he would.

"What can I say? You're finally getting what you want. Everything is falling into place."

"Yes, it is." I ignored the pangs in my heart and the despair in my soul. For some reason it didn't feel as good as I'd always thought it would. "I'm so close to getting what I wanted."

"So she's going to marry you?"

"Yup, she's going to marry me." I tried to forget the look on her face as she'd uttered the words I'd been waiting to hear. I should have been happy. I should have been over the moon at what I'd accomplished.

"Your father would have been proud of you."

"Thanks. I'm doing this for him." I closed my eyes and sighed as I thought about my dad. "You know that, right uncle?"

"I know. I understand why." He sighed. "You're like a son to me."

"You're like a dad to me. You know that," I whispered into the phone. "I know that you wish things were different, but you'll always be my second dad. I'll always think of you as Father."

"My brother would have been happy to hear that." He sighed.

"I'm so close now. His death won't be in vain."

"You're sure this is the move you want to make?"

"I'm sure." I nodded and hung up the phone. I walked over to my desk and opened the folder I had on Brandon Hastings. I looked over everything again and felt my heart hardening. Yes, I was absolutely sure. Then an image of Nancy popped into my mind. Her eyes pierced my soul. All I could think about was the way she'd looked at me when I'd taken her virginity. I couldn't ignore the feelings of guilt and remorse that flooded me. She was a casualty of war. She was a casualty that had no idea that she was allies with the enemy. She was a casualty that could ruin everything. I closed my eyes and tried to forget what it'd felt like to fuck her. It had felt different. She was right. We had a connection. We had something that I'd never experienced before. I'd lied to her about so much, but I hadn't lied to her about how I felt about her. Part of me did want to be different for her. Part of me wanted to be a better man. Part of me was scared at the feelings that overcame me when I was with her. I hadn't accounted for the feelings and I wasn't sure how to put them to the side. I was too close to fuck everything up now. I couldn't let anything get in the way of the plan. Even if it meant I went down with the ship. I'd get my revenge if it was the last thing I did. Nothing and no one was going to stop me from achieving my goal. Not even Nancy. Her face and sweet, unsure smile filled my head and I knew that ruining Brandon would ruin her as well. My heart broke then. A heart I hadn't known existed. I'd gone too far. I knew it in the depths of my soul. I knew it as sure as the fires burned in hell. I knew it as sure as I knew that the only devil in the situation was me, and I wasn't about to change anything in the plan. No matter how I felt about Nancy.

CHAPTER EIGHT

Nancy

I never thought I'd become one of those girls who lost their minds once they had sex. I never thought I'd be one of those girls, but all I could think about was Jaxon and how he'd fit so perfectly inside of me.

Every minute of the day my thoughts revolved around him and my father. There was a hole in my heart. A hole that hadn't been filled when I'd become part of the family. No matter how much I'd tried to convince myself that I was okay, I was still bitter and depressed that he hadn't tried to find me. I wasn't utterly convinced that he would have bothered to find me if I hadn't come to the private club with Frank.

I tried to ignore the pangs of hurt and let myself think about Jaxon instead. He was so much better than I'd initially thought. He still had issues and I still didn't trust him 100%, but at least he was honest. And he was an excellent lover. I smiled to myself as I thought about how he made me feel. So wonderful and relaxed. I would enjoy being married to him for however long it lasted. I'd enjoy him teaching me all the kinky things he knew. I laughed as I thought about just how much I'd love that. It's weird how life can change in an instant. All of a sudden I didn't feel so alone. I knew that Jaxon had issues, but so did I. We both had problems related to our parents. But that didn't mean we couldn't work our way through them. The way I saw it we were birds of a feather. We were both cut out of the same cloth. Maybe, just maybe, if we got married, we'd both find what we'd been searching for our whole lives. I knew that I was a dreamer. I knew that sometimes life didn't live up to my expectations and hopes. I couldn't help that. I wanted the fairy tale. I wanted to be rescued. I wanted to look in a man's eyes and know that he loved me more than anything. I wanted to be his number one. I needed to be his number one. My mother had loved Brandon. My grandparents had loved my mother. Brandon loved Katie. Hunter hadn't even known I existed. I wanted just one person to look at me as their number one. I wanted Jaxon to look at me and realize that I was special to him. I was ashamed to admit it. Even to myself. It made me feel weak and pitiful, but it also made me feel alive. It gave me something to be hopeful about. There was a part of me that really wanted to be with Jaxon. Even on the train, when I hadn't even met him yet, I'd been drawn to him.

The knock made me jump up off the bed and run to my door.

"You're knocking again?" I asked softly after I opened the door.

"Well, you know." He shrugged and walked in. "Now I know you prefer that."

"You always knew that." I smiled at him and grabbed onto his arm.

"Well, now I care about your wishes." He grinned and closed the door.

"Oh, so you didn't care before?"

"Not so much." He laughed and pulled me towards me. "But now that your wishes are directly related to how lucky I'm going to get, I figured I should care."

"You're so transparent." I rolled my eyes and leaned forward to kiss him.

"Is that a bad thing?" His eyes twinkled as he kissed me back.

"No. I like you transparent."

"Did you tell your dad about the wedding?"

"No." I shook my head. "I'm going to tell him afterwards."

"Makes sense. I'll tell my dad afterwards as well." He nodded. "We can tell them both at the same time."

"They are going to be so pissed." I nibbled on my lower lip.

"That will be their problem." He shrugged. "I'm done playing these games just because my father wants me to."

"Yeah." I nodded. "It will feel good to not have to lie anymore. Well, not lie directly, I guess. It will feel good not to have to avoid telling the truth."

"We have to do what we have to do." He pulled me towards the bed to him. "No matter how bad it makes us feel inside when we lie, we have to do what's right."

"I just don't want to hurt anyone." I sighed.

"I don't think either of us wants to hurt someone we care about." He pushed me back on the bed. "However, sometimes the greater good means that there are casualties on the way."

"I don't want there to be any casualties."

"I know you don't." He brushed the hair away from my face. "You're a good girl. I'm not sure that I deserve to be with someone as good as you."

"I'm not that good," I replied, feeling pleased.

"Modest as well." He pulled his T-shirt off. "You're too good for your own good."

"No one ever said that to me before." I laughed and reached down and pushed my hand into his shorts. "Are you hard or just happy to see me?" I squeezed his cock, delighting in the sound of his groans as I felt him hardening in my hands.

"What do you think?" He grinned as he reached over and squeezed my breast.

"I think you're happy to see me." I laughed and pulled his shorts down. "Very happy, it seems."

"You like that, don't you?"

"Yeah, I kinda do." I nodded and lowered my head. "I really do." I took his cock in my mouth and sucked softly, bobbing my head up and down, taking him as far into my mouth as I could.

"You do that like a seasoned pro." He groaned and lay back on the bed.

"I'm not sure if that's a compliment." I looked up at him and smiled.

"It is." He pulled me up and pushed me down on the bed. "Let me get your panties off. I need you naked."

"Need, or want?"

"Both." He growled as he threw my clothes onto the ground. "Do you know how badly I want you?"

"I think I just might." I grabbed his hand and pushed it into my wet pussy. "As badly as this?" I moaned as I felt his fingers slip inside of me.

"Yes, as badly as that." He groaned and lay down on the bed. "Get on top of me."

"What?"

"It's time for you to learn a new move."

"New move?"

"I want you to ride me."

"Like a cowgirl!"

"Exactly like a cowgirl." He pulled me on top of him. "I want you to be my dirty cowgirl." He reached up and grabbed my breasts.

"Does that mean you're my dirty cowboy?" I positioned myself over his cock and started rubbing myself back and forth.

"It makes me your stud." He grabbed my hips and held me still. "And if you keep teasing me like that, I'm not even going to be able to stop myself from pushing myself inside of you."

"Shouldn't you get a rubber?" I looked at him for a few seconds and continued to slowly move my hips.

"Not this time. I want you to feel what it's like to fuck without a condom."

"Oh." I bit my lower lip. "I don't want to get pregnant."

"I'll pull out before I come." He smiled at me gently. "And hey, a baby would be a good reason to get married."

"I'm too young to have a child." I leaned down and kissed him. "Though I have to admit that makes me feel kinda good that you want to have a baby with me."

"I'd love to have a baby with you." His expression changed as he stared at me. "Though you're right, this wouldn't be the right time."

"I've still got to go to college first." I nodded and we both groaned as I gyrated my hips on top of him and the tip of his cock entered my pussy slightly.

"Where are you going?" He groaned as he played with my nipples.

"I don't know as yet." I sat forward slowly and then lowered myself on top of his cock. It felt so hard and long and I felt like I was being stretched to the max.

"Don't stop." He groaned and wiggled my hips back and forth.

"It won't fit." I groaned.

"Lean forward slightly." He guided my body towards him and I sank down further on his cock.

"Oh my God." I exclaimed as he filled me up.

"Move back and forth." He groaned as I moved on him. "And up and down."

I followed his directions hesitantly at first and then as it started feeling better and better, I started moving faster and faster.

"That's it." He groaned as I increased my pace. "Oh my, Nancy, don't stop." He stared up at me with dark eyes. "Whatever you do, don't stop."

"I won't." I moaned as I felt his cock hitting a certain spot. The spot felt like dynamite and I rode him quickly, hoping to have him rub up against me in that spot as much as possible.

"Touch yourself," he commanded as I moved back and forth.

"Huh?" I looked at him blankly for a second and he guided my fingers to my clit. "Touch yourself as you ride me; trust me, it will only make everything feel better."

"Okay." I rubbed myself lightly as I continued to ride him. I groaned as I arched my back and started to feel that I was about to orgasm. "Oh my." I cried out as I felt my whole body was about to explode. I closed my eyes and rode him faster, rubbing myself faster as well. "Jaxon," I screamed as I came. I opened my eyes and saw his eyes widen as he grabbed my hips.

"Shit." He groaned as his body twitched on the bed. "I'm coming." He moved my hips back and forth quickly and I could feel his sperm filling me up. Finally he let me go and I collapsed onto his chest.

"Shit." He rubbed my hair and my back as I kissed his cheek.

"What?"

"I forgot to pull out."

"It's okay." I kissed him on the lips. "It felt right. Whatever happens, happens." I smiled at him through sleepy eyes. Nothing mattered in that moment. Everything was alright in the world.

"You should be mad at me, Nancy." His hand caressed the curve of my ass.

"It's not your fault." I shook my head and ran my fingers down his chest. "We'll have to be more careful next time."

"You have too much faith in me." He shook his head. "You shouldn't..."

"Shh." I put my finger on his lips. "Don't say it. I trust you, Jaxon." I kissed him again. "There's something between us. Something intangible. We're in this together. We've both been manipulated by men that should love us. We're a product of our upbringing and environment."

"I'm flattered that you see the best in me, Nancy. I don't know that I deserve it."

"Oh, but you do." He cuddled up to me. "I see inside of you, Jaxon. You're just like me. You're hiding inside somewhere because you've been deeply hurt and never felt a true love."

"I don't believe in love." He shook his head and pursed his lips.

"I'm not talking about romantic love." I ran my fingers over his lips. "Though, that's a part of it. I'm talking about unadulterated, pure love. Being loved just for being you, with all your faults and idiosyncrasies. We're two peas in a pod, Jaxon. I trust you because I believe in you. I believe that at the end of the day, you have my back and you like me. You like me a lot. I know that because I like you. I really like you. I always had this dream that I'd meet someone and we'd be soul mates." I looked into his eyes. "Don't go all scared on me or anything, but I had this dream that I'd meet someone who understood me. I've always been a lonely soul, trying to figure out the world by myself. And I've always felt slightly lost. I guess that's why it was so easy for Frank to manipulate me and it was so easy for me to have a crush on Hunter. But with you, I don't feel lost anymore. I don't feel like I have to pretend to be someone I'm not. I can be me. I can tell you how I feel. I can tell you what I'm thinking and you can do the same. We can both be real with each other. Neither of us is perfect. Neither of us knows what's going to happen, but we can figure it out by ourselves. We can do this. We can really do this, Jaxon." I grabbed his hands and held them in mine. "For so many years I've doubted myself and my thoughts. I've been scared to know who to trust and what to do. The first person I ever met who made me believe in myself was Meg. She saw something in me, she liked me and she treated me as an equal. I'll always love her for that. However, at the end of the day, she has a best friend. She has someone who holds her in high regard. You and me, we're loners. We play by ourselves. Well, Jaxon, we don't have to be loners anymore." I snuggled up next to him and stroked his face.

He looked back at me with a sad expression that made me wonder if he'd just heard what I'd said.

"I trust you and I want you to know that I think coming to the Lovers' Academy was the best decision I've ever made in my life." I took a deep breath then, not wanting to overwhelm him. I could see from his face that he was taken aback. A part of me wondered if I'd come on too strong. Maybe I'd scared him? I swallowed hard as I waited for him to respond. I needed to know that he felt the same as I did. It didn't matter what trials were put in front of us as long as we had each other. I really and truly believed that.

"Thank you." He said finally, his eyes bright, but his face not as excited as I'd hoped. "You're one of a kind, Nancy. You're truly one of a kind."

CHAPTER NINE

Jaxon

The day of the wedding was bright and sunny. It belied the dark and cloudy feelings I held inside. I wasn't happy and I wasn't excited. Nancy had agreed to go to a local courthouse with me. A local priest was going to come in and do a quick service. I should have felt happy that I was finally getting vengeance for my father. Ever since he'd killed himself, I had vowed to take down Brandon Hastings. If it hadn't been for Brandon buying his company and putting him out of business, he never would have committed suicide. I hated Brandon with everything that I had. I'd grown up knowing that I would do anything to bring him down. I knew that my father, as I called my uncle now, was disappointed in my actions. I knew that he didn't want me to go after revenge, but I also knew that he understood.

I picked up the phone to call him before I went to leave the room.

"Hey," he answered quietly, almost somberly.

"Hey," I repeated.

"So you're on your way."

"Yes." I nodded, even though he couldn't see me. "We should be married within a few hours. Then she'll become a Cade and I will become a legal member of the Hastings family, via marriage."

"How long will it take you to gain control?" he asked me quietly.

"I'll get a seat on the board of Hastings Corporation within a month once I'm a legal part of the family. There's nothing Brandon can do to stop me."

"I can't believe that his grandfather set it up like that."

"He wanted to make sure that the business remained a family business." I smiled. "I'm here to make sure that it remains a family business as well, until every last dime is gone."

"You don't have to do this, Jaxon."

"I do." I sighed. "I'll text you when you can let Hunter go."

"He's been a nuisance." The man sighed. "I wouldn't be surprised if he goes to the police and says he was kidnapped."

"Don't worry about it. I have a file full of papers on him. If he knows what's good for him, he won't go anywhere but home."

"I can't believe you got everyone to believe he was dead."

"No one actually asked to see a body." I shrugged. "You fired those two shots outside. Bobby showed up pretending he was a cop and I told Louise a story and she took it from there. You know women, they love a good gossip."

"It worked perfectly." He sighed. "I was waiting for someone to ask to see the body, but nobody did. I was hoping that would put a stop to the madness."

"It worked out perfectly. It was the seed of doubt I planted in Nancy's head about her father being the murderer that made her start to doubt herself."

"You ruined that girl's relationship with her father, Jaxon."

"It's fine." I sighed, trying to ignore the guilt. "I told her I thought it was you, after all."

"Why do you have to keep lying?"

"It was the only way, you know that. You know I love you, but what Brandon Hastings did was wrong. Yeah, so Dad wasn't in the best business. That was no excuse for Brandon to ruin his life. All he does is ruin lives. Now I'm going to ruin his."

"What about Nancy?"

"What about her?" I ignored the dart of pain that sprang through my heart. "This isn't about her."

"You don't think she's going to be hurt?"

"She'll be fine, especially when she realizes that Hunter is still alive."

"You know that girl doesn't care about him." He sighed. "And even after my coaching, it was pretty obvious for all to see that Hunter doesn't remember her."

"He was an idiot." I sighed. "It was a mistake to keep him around for so long, he nearly blew the whole thing."

"You needed him to set the whole thing in action."

"That's true. He and Frank will be rewarded." I nodded grimly. "Without Frank, none of this would have been possible."

"I know. I owe him a lot."

"And Nancy owes him nothing."

"We're getting what we've always wanted."

"This isn't what I wanted, Jaxon. I never wanted this." I knew he was tired and frustrated.

"I've come this far. I'm not backing out now." I hung up the phone and ignored the dart of anxiety that shot through me. I couldn't doubt myself now. I hadn't hurt anyone. I hadn't killed someone. I'd told a few lies. A few lies and that was it. I was nearly a part of the Hastings Corporation. Once I married Nancy, I'd be in. I could bring down the whole family. I'd ruin

Brandon as he'd ruined my dad. I smiled bitterly at the thought of how easy it had been to distract him. He was so blinded by his love for Katie that he'd backed off as soon as I'd told him that I'd tell her the truth about why our relationship had ended. He'd even believed that I'd gotten Nancy pregnant. If he'd done any digging at all, he would have known that Katie wouldn't have cared and Nancy and I hadn't even slept together yet. That was why it had been so important for me to put doubts in Nancy's mind. I couldn't have her talking to her father. She needed to doubt him. I didn't even need to have her believe my story 100%. I'd just needed her to believe it enough to ensure that she needed time to think and process.

Everything had worked so perfectly. Maybe too perfectly. Nancy had complete and utter trust in me. She believed that I was a lost soul. She believed that I could be saved. I suppose it was her youth. She was too young to understand that sometimes people were just bad. I felt horrible that I was the one who was imparting this knowledge to her, but she had to learn at some point. I walked to the door and stopped. I thought about what my uncle had said. I didn't have to go through with this. I could back out now. I could make up some excuse and just leave it alone. I opened the door slowly and walked down the stairs and waited for Nancy. I couldn't afford to be weak now. I'd come too close to change my plans at the last moment.

My heart stopped beating when Nancy walked down the stairs. She looked even more beautiful than I'd imagined she'd look. She looked like an angel all in white. I couldn't believe that she'd found a wedding dress so quickly. Though, she wasn't a bridezilla, so I shouldn't have been shocked that she'd found something she'd liked at the first store she'd entered.

"You look beautiful," I whispered up at her and she smiled at me with wide, happy eyes.

"You look very handsome, Jaxon." She grabbed my hands and held them in hers. "You look very, very handsome."

"Let's go do this thing." I frowned and turned away from her. I didn't need her making me feel bad. Already, I was started to feel funny inside. This whole situation didn't feel right. I didn't feel right. All I could think about was the conversation we'd had a couple of days previous about how much she trusted me and how happy she was now that she didn't have to feel alone. We drove to the courthouse in silence, both of us thinking our own thoughts about what was going to happen.

I looked over at her as we got out of the car and she gave me a small, awkward smile. It took me back to the first time I'd seen her on the train. She was vulnerable. She wanted to be loved. She was a wounded butterfly. As we walked to the courthouse I knew that there would be no turning back for me if I went through with the wedding. As she kept giving me small smiles and quick, furtive glances, I realized that Nancy was truly excited. She was truly excited and she was falling in love with me. I knew it as well as I knew my own name. I knew that her heart was beating to a different beat because my heart was as well. I had fallen in love with her. I'd tried to deny it. I didn't want it. I didn't deserve it, but I was in love with her. There was no way that I couldn't love her. She'd given herself to me in every way and she'd believed in me, when everything told her not to. She loved me and I loved her and this was our wedding day and the most ironic part of it was the fact that loving her meant I had to walk away. It just didn't seem fair, that I'd come this far and I was damned if I did and damned if I didn't. If I married Nancy, it would signal the end of her father's company, because I was going to take it down. She'd hate me and feel used and we'd both be heartbroken. If I walked away, it would mean that I loved her enough to not bring her father down, but then she'd be so heartbroken by my rejection that it would be over either way. I had two choices and both of them were awful. It came down to what I wanted most. Did I want to honor my father's name and bring down the man responsible for his death, or did I want to honor my heart and my love for Nancy and walk away because I knew that was best for her? I was minutes away from being married to her and I had no idea what I was going to do.

***

"Do you take Nancy Hastings to be your lawfully wedded wife?" The priest spoke loudly and clearly, nodding at me with a small smile as he waited for my answer. I stared at him for a second, my voice mute and my heart beating. I knew that whatever I decided to do would mean the downfall of someone.

As I stood there, I thought to myself that the question shouldn't be what would you do for love? The question should be what wouldn't you do? What wouldn't you do means a whole lot more. Trust me, I know. For love I'd walk to hell and back. I'd climb a mountain. I'd swim an ocean. I'd jump over valleys and swing through jungles. For love, I'd give my life. But that's not the question upon me now. The question upon me now is, would I walk away? Would I leave her standing at the altar because I love her? Did I love her enough to not marry her? That, my dears, is the ultimate question and I had no idea what to do.

I looked at Nancy then, standing in her white wedding dress, and I knew in that moment that marrying her wouldn't be right. It would be the ultimate betrayal of everything I stood for and everything she'd given me.

"No," I spoke loudly and clearly. I could see the shock in the priest's face and the hurt in Nancy's eyes. "No," I said again and took a step back. "I can't marry you, Nancy. I'm sorry." I hurried out of the courthouse then, my heart pounding and my head racing. I had to leave. I had to leave now and never come back. All I could see was the hurt expression in her eyes. I wanted to tell her why. I wanted to tell her the truth, but I knew that would mean nothing. The truth was even worse. To know that she'd put her faith and trust in someone who had lied to her the whole time, would be the nail in my coffin. I had to leave. That was all I could do. I had to leave and hope that her memories of me would be positive ones at the end of the day. I had to pray that I hadn't broken her. I wouldn't be able to live with myself if I'd broken her. I knew as I ran down the street that revenge didn't mean anything when it came to true love. True love and the heart of someone special would always be more important. I only hoped that I hadn't learned my lesson too late. I knew my heart would be forever broken. I only hoped that I hadn't ruined Nancy's trust and faith in humanity forever.

CHAPTER TEN

Nancy

Two Months Later

"I don't want you to go to college." Harry grabbed my hand as we walked into my dorm room. "I want you to stay at home."

"I know but I'll be home soon." I picked him up and hugged him. "I promise I'll call and I'll visit you."

"I love you, Nancy." He kissed my cheek. "I don't want you to go." His eyes grew wide and his lips started to pucker.

"I know, baby." I sighed and handed him to Katie who smiled at me sweetly.

"Let me walk you guys outside." I looked at my dad and Katie and they nodded. I knew that they were hesitant to leave me here by myself. I knew that they were worried about me, especially my dad. He had so much guilt about what happened with Jaxon. And he had so much guilt about how he'd abandoned me growing up. Some days it helped to know he felt bad, but other days it didn't stop the gnawing pain. My therapist said that was normal. She said that this wasn't an issue that was just going to go away. She'd even spoken to Brandon. She told him that he needed to understand that his actions had truly hurt me and that even though he was in my life now, there were 18 years that he'd missed and we'd never be able to get that back. He'd cried then. He'd cried and I'd cried and we'd hugged.

I knew he was sorry for what had happened and I knew that he loved me, but it still didn't fill the void. I hadn't told them everything that had happened with Jaxon. I still didn't really understand what had happened, but he'd just disappeared. It was almost like that whole situation had been a dream. I told Meg some of it and she'd hugged me. She'd told me I'd meet plenty of boys in college. What could I say to that? I didn't want to meet other men. I just wanted the one man. I wanted Jaxon. I took a deep breath as I walked out to the car with my family. I didn't want to think about Jaxon, this was a new start for me. I'd been wrong about him. He wasn't the one. He wasn't my soul mate. I had to live with that.

"Call me if you need anything, okay?" Brandon hugged me and I hugged him back, kissing him on the cheek as he held me close to him. He'd asked me a couple of questions about what had happened with Jaxon. He'd mentioned something about a baby and marriage. I'd laughed it off and he hadn't asked much else. It had hurt that he hadn't tried to pry more. It was just a further indication that his love for Katie was greater than his love for me. I tried to ignore the pain that came whenever I thought about how much he loved Katie. I wasn't even jealous of the fact. Not really. I just wished that I had it myself. I wished that Jaxon and I had that love. I wanted him to want me more than life itself. I sighed again as I waved Brandon, Katie, and Harry off. I needed to get over it. I didn't have Jaxon and I never would.

I walked back to my dorm room slowly, feeling sorry for myself. I should have been excited that I was starting a new journey in my life, but I wasn't. I wasn't excited at all. All I could think was, this is it, this is the rest of my life and I'm never going to be as happy or as excited as the time I was at the Lovers' Academy. I walked into my room and sat on my bed and stared at my suitcase. I knew I should start unpacking before my roommate got there.

KNOCK KNOCK.

"Coming." I sighed and walked over to the door. I plastered a smile on my face, ready to meet my new roommate. "Hi, I'm Nancy," I said as I opened the door.

"Hi, Nancy." His eyes were dark and he wasn't smiling, yet he still looked wonderful.

"Jaxon." I looked at him in shock. "What…"

"You like it when people knock first, right?" He gave me a small smile and walked into the room.

"I didn't think I'd see you again," I whispered as I stared at him in shock. "You just left me at the altar."

"I left you because I loved you."

"That makes no sense." I shook my head, my heart beating fast. "You should leave." I took a step away from him. I couldn't do this again. I couldn't play this game.

"I can't leave, Nancy." He took a step towards me and smiled.

"Why not?"

"I can't leave because I'm your teacher." He grinned and lightly touched my face. "As your teacher, I have to continue with your lessons until I'm sure you're ready to graduate."

"What happens when I graduate?" I whispered.

"When you graduate, you marry me." His hands ran across the top of my head.

"Are you sure?"

"I've never been more sure of anything in my life." He nodded, his eyes full of love and devotion. My heart melted as I saw his look. It was the same look that my dad gave Katie whenever he saw her.

"I guess I'd be down for one class." I smiled weakly, still unable to believe that he was here.

"I'm glad to hear that." He grinned and pulled a piece of rope out of his pocket. "I've got a very special class planned for tonight, if you're willing."

"I'm willing." I nodded eagerly. "I'm very willing."

"And that's why I love you, Nancy." He kissed my lips lightly. "You were right, you know. We are soul mates and we were made for each other."

"Shh." I grinned and kissed him back. "We can talk later."

"What would you like to do now?" He cocked his head and studied my face.

"I'd like to have my lesson." I grinned at him and he grabbed me around the waist and pulled me towards him. It was in that moment that I understood what everyone talked about when they talked about love. Love was never just simple and straightforward. The trials in love were many, but ultimately, at the end of the day, if you had the right partner, all the heartache was worth it.

The End

There will be one last book tying up Nancy's story and The Ex Games and The Private Club.

AUTHOR'S NOTE

Thank you for purchasing a J. S. Cooper book. If you enjoyed it, please leave a review on Amazon, Barnes & Noble, iTunes or Kobo.

Please join my mailing list to be notified as soon as the second book is out: http://jscooperauthor.com/mail-list.

Thank you for reading and purchasing this book. I love to hear from readers so feel free to send me an email at jscooperauthor@gmail.com at any time.

You can also join me on my Facebook page: https://www.facebook.com/J.S.Cooperauthor.

LIST OF AVAILABLE J. S. COOPER BOOKS

You can see a list of all my books on my website: https://www.facebook.com/J.S.Cooperauthor.

Rhett

Everlasting Sin

The Ex Games

The Private Club

After The Ex Games

The Love Trials

The Forever Love Series

The Last Boyfriend

Scarred

Healed

Crazy Beautiful Love

Finding My Prince Charming

Illusion

Guarding His Heart

The Only Way

If Only Once

To You, From Me

Redemption

Taming My Prince Charming

LIST OF BOOKS AVAILABLE FOR PREORDER

ILLUSION

The day started like every other day...

Bianca London finds herself kidnapped and locked up in a van with a strange man. Ten hours later, they're dumped on a deserted island. Bianca has no idea what's going on and her attraction to this stranger is the only thing keeping her fear at bay.

Jakob Bradley wants only to figure out why they've been left on the island and how they can get off. But as the days go by, he can't ignore his growing fascination with Bianca.

In order to survive, Bianca and Jakob must figure out how they're connected, but as they grow closer, secrets are revealed that may destroy everything they thought they knew about each other.

TAMING MY PRINCE CHARMING

When Lola met Xavier, Prince of Romerius, she was immediately attracted to his dark, handsome good looks and sparkling green eyes. She spent a whirlwind weekend with him and almost fell for his charm, until he humiliated her and she fled.

Lola wasn't prepared to find out that Xavier was her new professor and her new boss. She also wasn't prepared for the sparks that flew every time they were together. When Xavier takes her on a work trip, she is shocked when they are mobbed by the paparazzi and agrees to go to Romerius with Xavier to pretend she is his fiancé.

Only Lola had no idea that Xavier had a master plan from the moment he met her. He wanted a week to make her his, so that he could get her out of his system. Only Xavier had no idea that fate had another plan for him.

GUARDING HIS HEART

Leonardo Maxwell was shocked when his best friend, Zane Beaumont fell in love and got married. While he is happy for his friend, he knows that he definitely doesn't want to go the love and marriage route. He knows that there is nothing that can come from either of the two.

When his father calls him and tells him that it's time for him to take over the family business, he does so reluctantly. He's never liked the attention he gets as a billionaire's son, but he knows it's his duty.

Leo is not prepared for the animosity that he gets from his new assistant, Hannah on his first day of work. He has no idea why she hates him, but he's glad for it. He doesn't have time to waste staring at her beautiful long legs or her pink luscious lips. As far as he's concerned they can have a strictly professional relationship. However, that all changes when they go on their first work trip together.

IF ONLY ONCE (THE MARTELLI BROTHERS)

It's the quiet ones that can surprise you

Vincent Martelli grew up as the quiet one in his family. While his brothers got into trouble, he tried to take the studious route, even though he always found himself caught up in their mess.

When Vincent is paired up with a no-nonsense girl in one of his classes, he is frustrated and annoyed. Katia is everything he doesn't want in a woman and yet, he can't seem to get her out of his mind.

Then Katia shows up at his house with his brother's girlfriend, Maddie and he finds himself offering her his bed, when her car breaks down. When Katia accepts he is shocked, but he vows to himself that he won't let down his walls. As far as he is concerned there is no way that he could date someone like her. Only life never does seem to go as planned, does it?

REDEMPTION

One fight can change everything

Hudson Blake has two weeks to get his best friend Luke ready for the fight of his life. If Luke wins the championship he will receive one million dollars to help out the family of the woman he loved and lost.

Hudson's girlfriend, Riley doesn't want Hudson or Luke to fight and so she enlists the help of her best friend, Eden. However, Riley didn't count on Eden finding a battered and bruised Luke sexy and charismatic.

Luke has never felt as alive as he does practicing for the championship. He has vowed that he is not going to let anything get in his way. He knows that he is fighting for redemption and love. And he can't afford to lose.

THE ONLY WAY

Jared Martelli is the youngest Martelli brother, but he's also the most handsome and most confident. There is nothing that gets in the way of what he wants and he has no time for love.

Jared blows off college to start his own business and it's his goal to make a million dollars within five years. He's happy working hard and playing the field. That is until he meets Pippa one night at a bar. Pippa is headstrong, beautiful and has absolutely no interest in him. And that's one thing Jared can't accept.

He decides to pursue Pippa with plans of dropping her once she submits to his charms. Only his plans go awry when he realizes that Pippa has plans of her own and they don't include him.

TO YOU, FROM ME

Sometimes the greatest gifts in life come when you least expect them

Zane Beaumont never expected to fall in love with Lucky Morgan. He never expected to have a household full of children. He never knew that his life could be so full of laughter and love.

To You, From Me chronicles Zane and Lucky's relationship from the good times to the bad. It shows why marriage can be the best and worst experience in your life. Experience the gamut of emotions that Zane goes through as he goes through the journey of being a husband and father.

CRAZY BEAUTIFUL CHRISTMAS

Logan, Vincent and Jared Martelli decide to spend Christmas together with the women they love. Only none of their plans are going right. When they find a pregnancy test all three of them start to panic about becoming a father. Only they don't know which one of them is the daddy to be.

Join the Martelli Brothers on their quest for the perfect Christmas holiday. They may have a few more bumps in the road than they planned, but ultimately it will be the season of giving and loving.

ABOUT THE AUTHOR

J. S. Cooper was born in London, England and moved to Florida her last year of high school. After completing law school at the University of Iowa (from the sunshine to cold) she moved to Los Angeles to work for a Literacy non profit as an Americorp Vista. She then moved to New York to study the History of Education at Columbia University and took a job at a workers rights non profit upon graduation.

She enjoys long walks on the beach (or short), hot musicians, dogs, reading (duh) and lots of drama filled TV Shows.

Made in the USA
Lexington, KY
10 May 2016